For my mother, for asking the question that planted the seed,
and for my children, who knew the answer before it was asked —J.P.-M.

For the gnomes who live in my house —P.B.

Text copyright © 2019 by Jessica Peill-Meininghaus
Jacket art and interior illustrations copyright © 2019 by Poly Bernatene
All rights reserved. Published in the United States by Crown Books for Young Readers,
an imprint of Random House Children's Books, a division of Penguin Random House LLC,
New York. Crown and the colophon are registered trademarks of Penguin Random House LLC.

Visit us on the Web! rhcbooks.com
Educators and librarians, for a variety of teaching tools, visit us at RHTeachersLibrarians.com

Library of Congress Cataloging-in-Publication Data
Names: Peill-Meininghaus, Jessica, author. | Bernatene, Poly, illustrator.
Title: I'm a gnome! / Jessica Peill-Meininghaus; illustrated by Poly Bernatene.
Other titles: I am a gnome!
Description: First edition. | New York: Crown Books for Young Readers, [2019] | Summary: A gnome offers to show the
reader the way to the annual Gnome Festival, and points out along the way how gnomes differ from other magical
woodland creatures. Identifiers: LCCN 2018050335 | ISBN 978-1-5247-1984-5 (hc) | ISBN 978-1-5247-1985-2 (glb) |
ISBN 978-1-5247-1986-9 (epub) Subjects: | CYAC: Gnomes—Fiction. | Fairies—Fiction. | Humorous stories.
Classification: LCC PZ7.1.P4445 Im 2019 | DDC [E]—dc23

MANUFACTURED IN CHINA
10 9 8 7 6 5 4 3 2 1 First Edition
Random House Children's Books supports the First Amendment and celebrates the right to read.

I'M A GNOME!

by
Jessica Peill-Meininghaus

illustrated by
Poly Bernatene

♛

Crown Books for Young Readers
New York

HEY, YOU!

I bet you're looking for the annual Gnome Festival.
Don't worry, I can show you the way. I'm a gnome.
Say it with me: *gnome*.

It's spelled

but don't ask me why the *G* is silent,
because I have no idea!

Oh, don't shuffle your feet. We don't have time for that sort of flumadiddle! There's a party to get to, and they certainly won't wait for us. Follow me!

What are you doing? That's not the Gnome Festival. Those are elves. Don't you know how to tell the difference between one magical creature and another?

Even though elves and gnomes both like
hanging out in the forest, gnomes are *not* elves.

We just aren't!
This is an elf. Look at him.

Go ahead and wave. He's friendly.
Elves crack jokes and have pointy ears.
And just look at his striped leggings.

Do you see me wearing stripes?
Okay, maybe sometimes. But
long johns don't really count.
Neither do bathing suits. Anyway,
that's beside the point!
Gnomes aren't elves.

This guy here, *he*'s an elf.

E-L-F!

Now say goodbye. We don't have all day!

Where do you think you're going?

That's not the Gnome Festival!

That's a cave. Do you know who hangs out there?

D-w-a-r-v-e-s.

That's right, *not* gnomes.
And this fellow here is a dwarf.
He uses a pickax to mine
things like gold and gems.

Stay out of his way. He's working and, oh my,
will he be grumpy if you interrupt him.

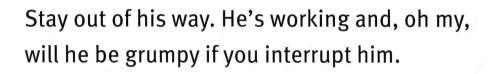

We gnomes don't do things like mining, and we definitely don't use pickaxes.

Well . . . hmm . . . okay, there *was* that time when my uncle Finklewink got stuck between some boulders while trying to harvest pebbleberries, and we had to use a pickax to get him out. But that doesn't really count. And whatever you do, don't tell him I told you that!

Anyway, as I was saying, those are dwarves.

Come on! If you don't get moving, you're going to make me late!
You never want to be late to the Gnome Festival.

You might want to hold your nose for this part of our journey.
No, of course this is not where the Gnome Festival is!
See this swamp? This is the sort of place trolls like.

You heard me. **T-r-o-l-l-s.**

They hang out under bridges and gather rocks for building.
Trolls have wild hair and eat skunk cabbage porridge.

We gnomes don't hang out in swamps.

Well, okay, if you're going to get technical, maybe *sometimes* we hang out in swamps, but only when we're invited to a cookout or a picnic. And we'd never eat skunky porridge. Why, just last week Jambalaya Gatorsmith had a barbecue, and we roasted mushrooms and toadstools and—

Oh, never mind all that!

Gnomes aren't trolls.
Our hair is not wild.

Okay, maybe *sometimes*.

But that doesn't matter!

We are gnomes, for goodness' sake!

Come along. We're going to miss the festival!

Why are you slowing down again?

The festival is definitely not in that brook over there.

See how it's all twinkly and sparkly?

That's because there are fairies there,

and if there is one thing we are not, it is fairies.

That's right. **F-a-i-r-i-e-s.**

They can fly while doing magic *at the same time*.

Gnomes don't fly. We fall. Really fast.

Luckily, we also bounce.

Sure, *sometimes* we hitch a ride with a bird, and technically that's *flying,* but that doesn't happen nearly as much as we'd like it to!

Just look at the way those fairy folk flit through the air! We are far too clumsy to be fairies.

Which brings me back to my point: we are gnomes.
We have round, jiggly, piggly bellies, twinkling eyes,
and big, fluffy white beards.

Okay? Except for the females! And the kids, of course!

GNOMES!

We made it! Just look at all these gnomes!
Now you can see how different we are from
elves and dwarves and trolls and fairies.

Do you see any gnomes wearing stripes?

Uh, perhaps that's not the right question.

Well, nobody has a pickax around here, right?

Hmm, scratch that one, too.

Wild hair! Definitely no wild hair here.

Oh, wait a minute. Forget that.

At least there is absolutely no one flying about. . . .
Argh! Oh, never mind!

I guess when it comes to gnomes, you should just look for a red pointy hat. We always wear those.

Okay, fine! Not *always*. . . . For goodness' sake, just

LEAVE US BE!